Have you read the other

Boyface books? ...

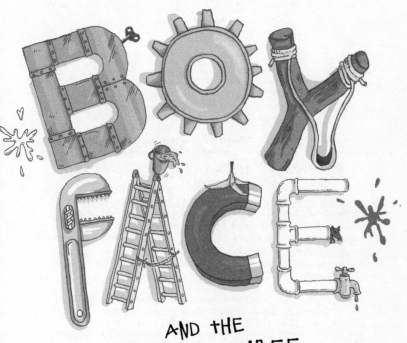

BOYFACE

AND THE POWER OF THREE AND A BIT

WRITTEN BY
JAMES CAMPBELL

ILLUSTRATED BY
MARK WEIGHTON

Hodder
Children's
Books

A division of Hachette Children's Group

For the Poyners, the Stirlings and the Hutchinsons, with
love, J.C.

For my darling Aunt Deirdre Czipri and Leo, with love,
M.W.

Text copyright © 2015 James Campbell
Illustrations copyright © 2015 Mark Weighton

First published in Great Britain in 2015
by Hodder Children's Books

The rights of James Campbell and Mark Weighton to be identified as
the Author and Illustrator respectively of the Work have been asserted by them
in accordance with the Copyright, Designs and Patents Act 1988.

A Catalogue record for this book is available from the British Library.

ISBN: 978 1 444 91806 9

Printed and bound in Great Britain by CPI Group (UK) Ltd, Croydon, CR0 4YY

MIX
Paper from
responsible sources
FSC
www.fsc.org
FSC® C104740

The paper and board used in this book are made from wood
from responsible sources.

10 9 8 7 6 5 4 3 2 1

Hodder Children's Books
An imprint of Hachette Children's Group
Carmelite House, 50 Victoria Embankment
London, EC4Y 0DZ
An Hachette UK company
www.hachette.co.uk

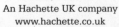

Contents:

STRIPE ONE

SOME time about now, or maybe a little time ago. Somewhere around three-quarters of the way between your next trip to the dentist and the time you did that silly thing with your bicycle and the trampoline. Yes, that's it. About then. Well, around about then, there was a village.

The village of Stoddenage-on-Sea was on the coast in a beautiful area of shingly beaches, pebblish coves and sandy cliffs that towered over the waves like wavy towers, waving at each other and saying things like, 'Hey! You're a cliff, I'm a cliff. We're a pair of cliffs. That's so cool. Maybe we should get together and talk about being cliffs. Oh, no. We can't because there's a village between us. Never mind. Let's just wave.'

For many years, the village had been a happy place where people would roll around giggling or screaming because someone had mentioned a hat or thought about a lemon meringue pie. Underwater singing seadonkeys had watched the villagers going about their happy lives, coming ashore at night to move rusty containers around.

For the last month, however, things had been very different. For a whole month, something had been wrong. For a whole month, Mr Antelope had been missing. Mr Antelope was, of course, Boyface's dad. It was he who had been teaching Boyface the ways of a Stripemonger: how The Machine worked, and how to take the stripes off one thing and stick them on another. Up until recently, a lot of the business had involved zebras. Boyface and his dad would have great fun taking the stripes off a zebra and selling it to people at the local riding school. Just over a month ago, things had gone terribly wrong when the local villain (Fibbernitchy, the weird-clown-boy) had started feeding oranges to the ponies that used to be zebras. The colour of oranges is the one colour that The Quantum Chromatic Disruption Machine cannot handle, so the ponies started to have all sorts of problems. Meanwhile, Mr Antelope had gone down to the pier – where the zebras were delivered – to see if he could find out what was wrong with them. And since then, no one in Stoddenage-on-Sea had seen him.

The whole village had been affected by Mr Antelope's disappearance. Folks who usually spent their days giggling and smiling would suddenly burst into tears or stare into space like mad sailors. The seagulls were still shouting at each other but now it sounded more like they were asking questions. Questions like:

Where is Mr Antelope?

When will he come back?

Why have you got more chips than me?

No one knew where Mr Antelope had gone but a lot of people suspected it was something to do with Fibbernitchy. That was certainly Boyface's theory.

(AUTHOR'S NOTE: THE ANTELOPE FAMILY WEREN'T ACTUAL ANTELOPES, BY THE WAY. THAT WAS JUST THEIR NAME. SOME PEOPLE HAVE NAMES THAT ARE THINGS AS WELL. I ONCE MET A GIRL CALLED JASMINE AND SHE WASN'T A FLOWER. I ALSO MET A BOY CALLED CLOUD AND HE WASN'T FLOATING AROUND IN THE SKY. HOWEVER, THE OTHER DAY, I MET A TEACHER CALLED MISS CHURCH AND SHE DID HAVE AN EXTREMELY POINTY HEAD.)

Mrs Antelope was not doing very well without her beloved husband. Since they had been married they had always shared the same underpants because their bottoms were exactly the same shape and size. Now, Mrs Antelope had piles of superfluous stripy pants all with the name tag 'Antelope' stitched inside.

Since her husband had vanished, she had stopped going upstairs for a morning nap. 'There doesn't seem much point on my own,' she would sigh, if anyone asked.

Boyface's mum had also started spending more and more time stealing more and more bits of other peoples' houses. The Antelope family home was now about three times taller, nine times bigger and eighty-one times as complicated as it was before Mr Antelope went missing. It had spires and minarets bodged on top of pillars and walls, bannisters and buttresses, bannistresses and buttisters; all stolen from annoyed friends. No matter how big and impressive she made their home, however, it didn't make her feel any better. She still missed her husband.

Since his dad's disappearance, Boyface had been doing his best to be sensibly responsible and responsibly sensible, keeping the family business going. He now spent most of his time in The Shop. They called it The Shop because they had always called it The Shop. It was in The Shop that Boyface practised the ancient skills of Stripemongery.

Most of the business centred around zebras. Once every lunar month, a wooden crate would appear on the wobbly pier. Boyface never knew where it came from but it always contained five or six zebras.

Mr Pointless (the local delivery man) would then balance them on his shoulders and carry them up the hill, through the cobbled streets, to The Shop. Boyface had to unpack the zebras, feed them and settle them in to make them feel at home until it was time to remove their stripes.

His main Stripemongering tool was, of course, The Quantum Chromatic Disruption Machine. The Machine was magical and mystical, mysterious and elliptical and no one was really sure how it worked. Here is a list of some of the things it could do:

- Recycle homework into chicken nuggets

- Reduce holiday shirts to a manageable level

- Repair frogs

Neutralise wasps

Train bees to dance

Make toast

Predict avalanches, traffic jams and kittens with some accuracy

Make loo paper more interesting

Repair Budgies

Destroy Budgies

- Make budgies feel unsure of whether you like them or not

- Frighten goats

- Make helmets that protect you from weather

- Make helmets that protect you from meteor strikes

- Make helmets that protect you from dinosaurs

- Make helmets that protect you from helmets

Make helmets that tell you
when the list is long enough

All of these features were very different and involved various complicated combinations of levers and buttons, dials and matrices.

Boyface's dad had begun to teach him all of the different things you could do with The Machine but, in the last month, Boyface had been mongering stripes without any guidance. The result of this was that there had been a lot of disasters.

For example, one day, Boyface had the brilliant notion of self-replicating wallpaper. The idea was to take the growth molecules out of an artichoke plant and quantumly sew them onto some wallpaper. The theory was that you would only need to put up one roll of the new paper. Then you would sprinkle some water on it, stand back and watch it grow all over your walls until your living room was covered in a beautiful artichoke pattern. The project almost worked but when Boyface sold a roll to a lady called Diane McEndemol it turned her kitchen into an artichoke forest. She couldn't open her oven door for artichoke plants, and a load of rabbits moved in. Boyface hadn't expected that and Mrs McEndemol hadn't wanted it. So Boyface had to give her her money back, along with a suitcase of jelly babies as compensation.

Boyface's next business idea was quite revolting. He invented a Quantum Chromatic Face Mask. Various teenagers put the mask on their spotty faces, which was connected to The Machine in The Shop. With a couple of pulls of a

lever, a pre-programmed sequence would fire up and all the teenagers' spots would be removed. This could have been a genius idea, but Mrs Antelope suggested they use the spots they had taken off. So they put the spots on pizzas and tried to sell them to folks walking through the village. But no one ever bought the pizzas because they were revolting.

Also, once all five of the village's teenagers had had their spots removed, their faces were clean and clear. They consequently spent most of their evenings looking at themselves in the mirror and entering talent competitions on the telly. What they should have been doing, of course, was hanging out at the bus stop, mumbling to each other and freaking out old ladies. Because they weren't there, the bus-stop got sold for scrap to a man called Shiny Tanker who ran the scrapyard round the back of the village. This meant that the bus had no idea when to stop and on most days it just kept on going, ending up in the sea.

By far the most disastrous of Boyface's Stripemongering projects, however, was the case of Oswald Muesli. Oswald was a small, oily boy who happened to have two problems. The first was that his dog (a long-haired Stoddenage terrier) seemed completely unable to follow instructions. It wouldn't sit, roll over or fetch anything. It just bounced about and yapped like an angry yo-yo. Oswald's second problem was his little sister. Maximilliana Muesli was the most well-behaved child that had ever been invented.

'The problem is,' Oswald Muesli had explained to Boyface in a voice like a squirt of ketchup, 'she makes me look bad by comparison. I'm fed up with my mum going on about how perfect she is and I'm fed up with the stupid dog.'

Boyface drew up a Stripe Plan – like he did with all his customers – to solve Oswald's problems. The solution presented itself quite quickly. They would simply put Maximilliana and the dog into The Machine, take the obedience molecules out of the girl and then put them into the dog.

It all went a bit wrong. The dog was great. It would let itself be trained to do all sorts of tricks. Oswald was able to enter it into competitions and everything. Maximilliana, however, with none of her obedience, suddenly had no sense of what was right and wrong. She went from being the most well-behaved little sister in the world to being the naughtiest monster you could imagine. In the first week after the quantum transfer, she set fire to a wheelie bin, stole Mr Pointless' van and painted rude words on all the ponies at the riding school with gloopy white paint.

The words were so rude that they are too rude to print in a book.

Here are the words that she wrote:

🔘 Pooflip

🔘 Flumming blinger

🔘 Blinging flummer

🔘 Trump-bundle

🔘 Snot-crumble

🔘 Grembles

🔘 Blup

- Parp-snuffler

- Ankle-bracelet

- Feather-monker

- Gerbil-face

- Face-gerbil

- Snowtch

- Winkle-trap

- Austrian Hiccups

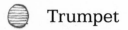 Trumpet

 Crumpet

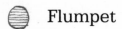 Flumpet

Wumpet

Thumpet

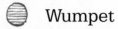 Bumpacket

Unexpected-Item-In-
Bagging-Area

Despite these catastrophes, Boyface was not put off being a Stripemonger. He simply had to keep the business going until his dad came back. Besides, he wasn't doing all this on his own. He had the Tartan Badger and his two best friends, Clootie Whanger and Entelechy Venn to help him. They were a gang.

Not everyone in the village was unhappy about Mr Antelope's vanishment. Up in the abandoned Ickle Chuff restaurant, Fibbernitchy was delighted about the situation.

He was also the only person in the village who knew exactly what had happened to Boyface's dad. He had used his mum's bank card to pay the seadonkeys to put him in a shipping container and take him away.

STRIPE TWO

One Sunday morning, the gang were hanging out on the pier that poked out into the harbour like a small dog's tail. Boats didn't tend to come in and out on a Sunday so they had the place pretty much to themselves. The sea was ever so slightly choppy, so the rickety old pier was rocking from side to side in a way that made the friends feel like they were on a ship, bound for distant lands.

Boyface had activated the Tartan Badger, turning it from the worst pet in the whole wild world into the most excitingly magical thing ever. The Tartan Badger was a portable version of The Quantum Chromatic Disruption Machine. It wasn't as powerful but you could take it on adventures. On its tummy were three hand-shaped patches, and the gang had worked out that if they each put a hand on one,

the Tartan Badger would look into their minds and turn on its bum projector.

It would hum in a strange electrical way and curl itself up into a mechanical doughnut shape. With a hydraulic lift of its tail, a bright blue light would shine out of its bum, a kind of cross between a projector and a virtual reality chandelier. It was the coolest thing in the whole wild world.

Over time they had begun to work out

what the projections were. They were usually a kind of three dimensional map which showed how things, places and people were connected.

On this particular Sunday morning, Boyface was trying to solve a problem involving the stripiness of bees. Clootie was hiding her face by wearing a cardboard box on her head. Entelechy was using the Tartan Badger to display a picture of dots of different colours and tones, using the side of one of the abandoned containers as a cinema screen.

The three friends were all committed to keeping the Stripemongering going. Entelechy had become amazingly useful at patterns and colours so he was really good at helping customers choose a design for their cat or what colour their guinea pig could be. Entelechy's two dads had bought a little shop in the village and were selling materials and notions and buttons and bangles and other haberdashery. Entelechy had started going to the local school

where he and Clootie would sit at the back, drawing circular diagrams of what colours go with other colours. Clootie would be hidden by her box and he would use his ability to sit very still in yoga poses, blending in with the collages and wall displays behind him.

Clootie's disguise had gone from a saucepan to a pillow case, and was now a cardboard box with holes in it. Entelechy's problem with the box was the colour. He wouldn't have minded if it was a more striking

colour that went with her school
uniform but it was just that normal,
buff beige box colour and it made
him feel slightly ill.

Boyface didn't really know anything
about colours but he sensed that
there was something important going
on with Clootie's box. Clootie had
told him months ago that the reason
she always had her face covered was
because of the bruises caused by
juggling accidents. But he had never
believed her. He closed his eyes and
wondered 'What would Dad do?'

The sea was sleepy and still and the village was still sleepy in a Sunday morning kind of way. Even the seagulls were keeping themselves to themselves. Boyface decided that this was as good a time as any to ask Clootie what the flumming bling was going on.

'Clootie,' he said softly. 'You are my friend and I love you. Will you take off the cardboard box?'

Clootie froze for a while. Entelechy tuned into the conversation and the three of them sat very still.

38

'If you really want me to...'

She carefully took the box off her head and placed it beside her. The sun seemed to blind her and she blinked a few times. Boyface and Entelechy looked at her face. It was a beautiful, gentle moon of a face – but there was something very odd going on with her hair. At first, Boyface thought that maybe her auburn locks had simply been squashed by the cardboard box – a terrible case of 'box hair' – but then he saw that

Clootie had had the most disastrous haircut ever.

Her fringe was at an angle and fell in many directions at once. There were tufty bits poking upwards like knitting needles and some of it didn't even look like it was hair at all. It was as if someone had cut Clootie's hair with a lawnmower. 'You didn't get that haircut from juggling, did you?' said Boyface.

Clootie bit her bottom lip and looked at her feet. 'No,' she said quietly.

So quietly that Boyface could hardly hear her. It was the quietest thing he had ever heard her say.

The three friends sat and looked out over the sea. None of them knew what to say. Even the Tartan Badger curled up in a ball and kept silent.

Clootie didn't want to talk any more. She picked up her cardboard box and got it back onto her head just before she burst into tears. Boyface listened to her sobs, squeaking from inside the box like unhappy bits of polystyrene packaging. He wished he knew how to make it better. He didn't want his friend to cry.

'I'm sure we can do something about it,' he said as cheerfully as he could. 'I could get my mum to look at it. Or we could take you to a hairdresser. Or Mandala at the cafe could make you a herbal remedy. You could live with us. Or when Dad comes back he could use the Quantum Chromatic—'

Clootie reached over and stopped him by putting her little finger on his knee. 'It's okay,' she said with a tremble. 'It'll grow out over time. There is nothing anyone can do.'

Boyface and Entelechy blinked at each other. They didn't understand. The Tartan Badger put his front paws over his eyes. 'And I can't move in with you,' continued Clootie. 'For a start, I really love my bedroom, and if I lived in your house, my hair would still have to live there too.'

And then Clootie burst into so many tears that Boyface thought they would all be washed off the pier and into the deep blue sea.

STRIPE THREE

The next day, Boyface was up early, working in The Shop. His mum was out on a stealing mission and Clootie and Entelechy were at school. The Tartan Badger was stretched out on his back on one of the orange plastic chairs, fast asleep and snoring like an angle grinder.

The Shop was very messy but Boyface knew exactly where everything was. Piles of boxes and crates towered above him, leaning towards each other like they were going to fall, papers and books and half-finished Stripe Plans covered the surfaces, along with unopened bills and hand-written lists of things to do, things to buy and things to be.

The place smelled of bicycles and rubber balls and particularly strong soap.

In the middle of The Shop was, of course, The Quantum Chromatic Disruption Machine in all its shiny, grimy, cranky gloriousness.

Boyface was looking into the observation panel. There was the mysterious circular rainbow with his shadow in the middle of it. The Machine seemed to be drawing in light from somewhere behind him and creating this wonderful spectrum of colours. Boyface narrowed his eyes and looked more closely at the strange blue curls of light that were

dancing and twisting from the shadow of his head. His dad had once told him that these were called Inklings.

Boyface picked up his notebook and flicked back a few hundred pages. There he had written:

The Inklings of The Machine are the forgotten adventures of dogs.

He still didn't know what this meant. He'd learned that the Tartan Badger might be one of those forgotten adventures but what were the others? Was his dad one of them or was he, Boyface, just a forgotten adventure of some dog somewhere? Would they help him find his dad? Boyface didn't really know.

The zebras arrived once every lunar month, always on the full moon. The most recent delivery had arrived about three weeks before, although Boyface hadn't managed to sell them all yet. A couple of the stripy pooflips were still in The Shop. Boyface had never seen who delivered them, they always arrived at the end of the pier in the middle of the night, to be found the next

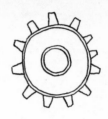

morning. Mr Antelope had always maintained that the zebras had been sent from somewhere called Tropical Antarctica but Boyface reckoned that sounded like a made-up place.

Boyface led one of the zebras from its shelf and carefully stuffed it into one of the input chutes of The Machine. A lady called Norberta Dentressangle had ordered a grey pony with funny-looking pink squiggles all over it. Boyface thought he had the skills to take the stripes off the zebra and apply a fancy pattern which

Entelechy had designed specifically for the job.

The zebra was quite a big animal and Boyface had to use the vertical and horizontal magnetwaffles to hold it in the right place. Once it was fixed he started to identify the stripes and tell The Machine what he wanted it to do. Just like his dad had taught him.

Once everything was set, Boyface pressed the RUN button and watched through the observation panel as the Quantum Chromatic Disruption

Machine bimbled and whirred, hummed and stirred and gradually erased the stripes from the zebra. As it did so, however, something extraordinary happened. It was like the Quantum Chromatic Disruption Machine was trying to tell him something. In the observation panel, Boyface saw the zebra melting away into swirling clouds of colour and dust. Boyface looked deeply into the rainbow fog trying to see patterns and shapes; to feel what The Machine was trying to say. Then he saw it. A beach. The beach of Stoddenage-on-Sea. Light was glinting off something

resting on the sand, making it difficult to see what it was. Boyface adjusted some of the The Machine's settings. It was a bottle – a bottle sitting among the pebbles of the beach. The zebra remained inside The Machine, unconcerned, held in place by the magnetwaffles.

Boyface knew exactly what to do. He put The Machine onto standby mode; picked up the still-sleeping Tartan Badger and ran out onto the street. A few dozen boy-sized strides later and he was on the beach.

The young Stripemonger activated the Tartan Badger to use as a kind of metal-detector. It wasn't tuned to look for coins and treasure though, it was set to find words, messages and bottles.

It didn't take long before the Tartan Badger was bimbling and whirring away like an enchanted washing machine. Then it pointed itself across the beach like an arrow.

Boyface found the bottle wedged between two large pebbles. Trembling

with excitement, he uncorked the bottle and read the message that was rolled up inside it. It must have been written with the tiny stub of a pencil that Mr Antelope always kept behind his ear.

BOYFACE!
IT'S YOUR DAD. I'VE BEEN KIDNAPPED BY BADDIES FOR SOME REASON. WHEN I WENT TO THE PIER, THEY JUMPED ON ME AND BUNDLED ME INTO AN OLD CONTAINER. I'M NOT SURE BUT I THINK THEY WERE SEADONKEYS. THEY CERTAINLY HAD VERY HAIRY FACES, I CAN TELL YOU. ANYWAY, THEY'VE STUCK ME IN THIS CRATE FULL OF OLD STUFF: BOTTLES

AND VEGETABLE PEELINGS AND PEOPLE'S
RECYCLING. 'PUT THAT CRATE ON THE NEXT
BOAT TO TROPICAL ANTARCTICA,' I HEARD
SOMEONE SAY.

I WAS SO SURPRISED I MUST HAVE FALLEN
ASLEEP. WHEN I WOKE UP, I WAS ON A BOAT.
I COULDN'T SEE, OF COURSE, THE ONLY HOLES
ARE RIGHT UP IN THE TOP OF THE CRATE.
I COULD TELL IT WAS DAYLIGHT BUT I HAD
NO IDEA HOW FAR FROM SHORE WE WERE
OR HOW LONG I'D SLEPT. I COULD HEAR THE
WAVES AND FEEL MYSELF SWAYING FROM
SIDE TO SIDE. I CAN ONLY ASSUME THAT I AM
HALFWAY TO TROPICAL ANTARCTICA BY NOW.

I HAVE BEEN LIVING ON MOULDY VEGETABLES AND THE DREGS AT THE BOTTOM OF MILK CARTONS. NONE OF THIS IS VERY NICE BUT STRIPEMONGERS CAN COPE WITH ANYTHING.

I HAVE BEEN WRITING NOTES, PUTTING THEM INTO BOTTLES AND THROWING THEM THROUGH THE HOLES IN THE TOP OF THE CRATE. I KNOW IT'S UNLIKELY BUT I HOPE ONE OF THEM FINDS ITS WAY TO YOU. IF YOU DO READ THIS PLEASE COME AND RESCUE ME. AND BRING FRIED EGG SANDWICHES. TELL MUM SHE IS LOVELY. THEN SERIOUSLY COME AND RESCUE ME. AND DON'T FORGET THE SANDWICHES; I'M STARVING!

'Flumming bum-packets!' said Boyface. His dad had sent him a message! The gang would have to launch a rescue mission.

Boyface ran as fast as he could to Stoddenage Primary School, and skipped over the back fence, up to the window of the classroom where Clootie and Entelechy were having a maths lesson. He tapped on the window to attract their attention, and using his incredibly expressive eyebrows, he told them what had happened.

Clootie and Entelechy waited for a suitable moment, then slipped out of the open window. The three of them ran back to The Shop to make a Stripe Plan.

STRIPE FOUR

'It's quite simple,' shouted Clootie from behind her cardboard box. 'We just need to go to Tropical Antarctica, find your dad and scrag the seadonkeys.'

'We're not scragging anyone,' said Boyface. 'We'll use my skills as a Stripemonger, Entelechy's almost-invisibility talents and your shoutiness. And we'll get Dad back!'

The gang thought about the problem. They had brought a map of the world with them, hoping to find where Tropical Antarctica was but it

MAP OF THE WORLD

didn't seem to be anywhere on the map at all. 'It must be some sort of secret place,' thought Boyface.

'Why don't we use the Tartan Badger?' suggested Entelechy.

The Tartan Badger let out a grumpy sigh but let Boyface turn it over and activate its projector. The three chums each put a hand on its belly. The creature whirred and clicked and light from its bum shone around the room, turning The Shop into a kind of three dimensional circus.

Suspended in the air were thousands of giggling balls of light. Boyface looked at them. He tried to watch the connections between the lights without concentrating too much. He saw himself in the projection, and his dad's face. All he had to do now was look at what was connecting them. He could feel the ends of his fingers and toes vibrating, and saw that Entelechy's and Clootie's were too. All three of them were looking for the connection, looking for the answer. Boyface saw it first. Hundreds of tiny zebras linking him to his dad. Galloping. Galloping backwards.

Boyface switched off the Tartan Badger's projector. The other two looked at him curiously. 'I think I've got it,' he beamed. 'I think I've got a Stripe Plan!'

The plan was simple and genius. If the zebras came to Stoddenage-on-Sea from Tropical Antarctica, all they had to do was follow the zebras backwards.

The full moon was due in a week, meaning a shipment of zebras wouldn't be landing on the pier until then. The gang's plan was to build a present in a massive crate. A present that they would leave on the pier. The crate would be labelled:

For the people of Tropical Antarctica.

A special thank you for all the zebras. Please take this crate back to Tropical Antarctica and don't open it until you get there.

Please.

Boyface, Clootie, Entelechy and the Tartan Badger would be hiding inside the crate. This way, whoever did the delivering of the zebras (they suspected it was the seadonkeys) would unknowingly take them to the mysterious land and they could rescue Mr Antelope.

It was a brilliant plan and they all knew it. All they needed to do was work out the details. They had just seven days. The three ten-year-olds and the Tartan Badger met the next morning at the pier, armed with

notebooks, colour charts and many many felt tip pens.

After a couple of hours they had worked out some of the problems. They now had ideas and answers for the following:

Where they would get the crate

How they would make the inside comfortable to be in

How they would get out in an emergency

What they would eat

What they would drink

How they would get the crate
to the end of the pier

The Stripe Plan was beautiful. It took
up a lot of paper and included ideas
from all of them.

'That just shows you how brilliant
we are together. It shows the
power of three,' said Clootie proudly.
She was quickly corrected, however,

by the Tartan Badger who bit her on the toe and looked intently into her eyes.

'Sorry,' said Clootie. 'Maybe I should have said the power of three and a bit.' They all giggled until Entelechy noticed that Clootie was bleeding and fainted.

'Are you poppinuponable?' shouted Clootie as she swaggered into Shiny Tanker's scrapyard. Shiny Tanker was relaxing in an old bath tub, balanced on a pile of tumble-dryers and bus-stops, eating a massive, juicy pear.

'Between the hours of eight in the morning and four in the afternoon,' he yawned, 'I am poppinuponable

73

and you and whoever are muchwelcomeable to pop in upon my scrapyard and look around for any old metaljunkable thingables you might like to buy for small amounts of bundlewodge.'

Clootie thought about what he had said for a few seconds and continued, 'I'd like to buy an old, metal crate please. The sort of thing you'd find on a cargo boat.'

Shiny Tanker pointed with his pear at a rusty coloured container on the

other side of the yard. It was about the size of a car. 'That would be perfect,' squealed Clootie. 'Is it expensive?'

'Dependables uponawot you wantage it for.'

'It's for rescuing Mr Antelope. We've had a message in a bottle from him asking us to go and get him.'

Shiny Tanker took another bite from the pear, wiped the juice from his lips with the sleeve of his boiler suit and said, 'Then you can have it for nothinguponit.'

'Thank you,' said Clootie, 'you are lovely!'

* * * * *

On the other side of the village, Entelechy Venn was having a nice pot of tea with his two dads: Daddy-This and Daddy-That. 'I don't know how long I'll be away for,' he twittered as he poured from the pot, as if it were normal for

ten-year-old boys to go on voyages to unknown lands. 'But it shouldn't be more than a couple of weeks. Just think of all the exotic fabrics I'll find in Tropical Antarctica. It'll be fabulous.'

Daddy-This and Daddy-That weren't quite sure but finally agreed that Entelechy could go on the rescue mission, as long as he brought back lots of exciting things to sell in their haberdashery shop. They gave him a big bundle of money. Entelechy couldn't believe his eyes. 'Thanks Dads,' he said with a gasp, stuffing

the notes into his bag. 'But there is one more thing … '

'What's that?' whistled Daddy-This.

'Could I have loads of cushions and throws and pashminas and pillows and scatter-buttons to make the inside of the crate a little more tolerable? Less utilitarian. More plushy.'

* * * * *

Back at Boyface's house, he and his mum were in the kitchen. Boyface

had the Stripe Plan in front of him and had just finished explaining it to Mrs Antelope, who was making a huge pile of disgusting-looking pancakes. There was a toilet on top of the kitchen table that hadn't been mentioned yet. Boyface hoped it had nothing to do with the pancakes.

'Thanks for making all these pancakes,' said Boyface lovingly. 'They'll keep us from getting hungry while we are on our way to Tropical Antarctica.'

'Anything to get my gorgeous husband back,' sighed Mrs Antelope. 'I do miss him.'

'Why is there a toilet on the table, mum?' asked Boyface.

'Well,' said his mum, rolling up her storytelling sleeves, 'you know when you're in someone's house and you ask if you can use the loo and they say "as long as you give it back", in a really annoying way?'

'Yes.'

'Well, I thought I would teach them a lesson.'

'Where will we put it?'

'It can go in the corner of the living room for emergencies.'

83

STRIPE SIX

On the day of the full moon, everything was ready. Mr Pointless had very kindly carried the crate on his head from Shiny Tanker's scrapyard to the end of the pier. The gang fitted it out to make it comfortable, filling it with plastic boxes of pancakes and elderflower cordial, and some artichokes for the Tartan Badger. As the sun went down and the big

round moon floated up from behind the towering cliffs, Boyface stood in front of The Machine. It was running a series of tests on a bucket of stripy sick, brought in by a dog that only ate bees. But Boyface wasn't really watching. He was already imagining travelling the waves and wondering what on earth was going to happen to him and the gang.

Boyface punched the series of buttons and pulled the sequence of levers that would shut The Machine down. This would be the last time he would switch it off until he came back from his adventure. One by one, the internal components of The Machine disabled themselves and softened. The noise became quieter. Gas releases popped and cooling fans slowed, idled and gave a final turn and squeaked to a stop. The Quantum Chromatic Disruption Machine was switched off.

Boyface wondered how long it would take to rescue his dad. He wondered how long it would be before Mr Antelope was back in front of The Machine. When it would be switched on again.

As he stood there, gazing at its knobbly magnificence, he felt the breath of his mum on his ear. She had crept up behind him and silently put her head on his shoulder. She smelled of butter and puppies. He sighed.

'Are you going to be all right while I'm gone?' Boyface asked her. 'You'll be on your own.'

'Yeah,' said Mrs Antelope. 'I'm planning to do a lot of stealing. Shiny Tanker has got a beautiful digger in his scrapyard and I'm thinking of pinching it and popping it up in the

attic. As a toy. It would be great for moving things around with.'

Boyface gently poked his mum in the ribs. He didn't like it when she talked about stealing. She made an 'oof' noise and giggled. Boyface felt her draw even closer to him and suddenly her big, bear-like arms wrapped him in a hug.

'Are you scared, Boyface?' Mrs Antelope asked her son. 'Nervous? Hungry? Trepidatious? Wobbly? Feeling out of your depth?'

Boyface thought for a moment. 'Dad told me once,' he said with a hum, 'that it's only when you're out of your depth that you really learn how to swim.'

Mrs Antelope let out an unexpected laugh that made her belly rumble and shudder against Boyface's shoulders. 'It wasn't him that said that,' she explained. 'It's true enough, but it wasn't your dad. It was me. And it wasn't you I was telling. It was him.'

Boyface wriggled out of the hug a little so he could twist round and look at his mum's lumpily lovely face. 'What do you mean?' he asked.

'It was when you were a tiny baby,' she told him. 'And he was in a bit of a panic.' (Boyface couldn't imagine his dad in a panic but he didn't interrupt). 'He was worried that he wasn't successful enough at Stripemongering to look after a baby. "I'm out of my depth," he said. So I told him that it's only when you're out of your depth ...'

' ... that you really learn how to swim,' completed Boyface.

'That's right,' said his mum. 'You must have been listening.'

'Of course I was listening,' beamed Boyface. 'That's what babies do.'

By now, The Machine was silent. 'I don't know how long I'm going to be, Mum,' said Boyface. 'I think it's best if The Shop is closed until I get back. I've made a sign.'

Boyface pointed to a big square of cardboard:

Closed Due To
Rescue Mission

Back As Soon
As We Can

Ten minutes later, Boyface was standing outside The Shop with a suitcase and a woolly hat. The Tartan Badger was sitting at his feet, a little closer to him than usual, looking up at him. Boyface fixed the sign to the door and locked everything. The keys went on a bit of string around his neck and he set off towards the pier to meet up with the gang, the Tartan Badger trotting at his heel.

STRIPE SEVEN

'I love the soft furnishings, Entelechy,' said Boyface. 'And the lighting is amazing.'

'Oh, it's nothing,' shrugged Entelechy. 'I just threw some things together and fluffed it up a little.'

The gang of three and a bit were now snugly inside the old crate, making

themselves comfortable amongst the cushions and scatter-buttons that Entelechy had borrowed from his dads' shop.

'Are you sure we can't get accidentally locked in?' asked Clootie, sounding a little scared.

'Of course not,' proclaimed Boyface. 'I've designed a fool-proof system.' Boyface was about to explain the system when he noticed that Clootie wasn't wearing her cardboard box, or a pillowcase or a saucepan.

PARP

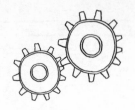

'You're not wearing anything over your face, Clootie,' he smiled.

'Yes, well, I thought that as we're having an adventure, it might be time to stop that sort of thing.'

Boyface and Entelechy beamed at her, and Entelechy proposed a toast with the elderflower cordial Mrs Antelope had made for them. The three and a bit munched their way through some of the disgusting pancakes, saving most of them as they had no idea how long their journey would be.

At the end of their meal, the gang went over the plan.

The Stripe Plan dictated that the gang stay awake so that they would know what was happening. But as night got deeper and quieter, the furnishings got softer and snugglier and their eyelids grew heavier and heavier and heavier.

Half asleep, Entelechy yawned to Boyface. 'You didn't tell us about your fool-proof plan to make sure we don't get locked in.'

'I put a sign on the outside of the crate,' said Boyface as he drifted off. 'It says, "Please Don't Lock This Lock, Or We Won't Be Able To Get Out".'

'That'll do it,' snored Clootie.

Half an hour later when they were all fast asleep, Maximilliana Muesli came tiptoeing onto the pier. She was still affected by the quantum transfer with her brother's dog and was having a very naughty night. So far, she had snuck out the back door of her house, frightened a hedgehog, let the tyres down on someone's bike and put a dead pigeon through Mr Pointless' letter box. Now she was prowling around the harbour thinking about untying a boat or something.

She saw the rusty old crate on the end of the pier. 'What the pooflip is this?' she said to herself as she read the sign. 'Please don't lock this lock?' She grabbed hold of the lock and clicked it into place. Cackling to herself she went home to flood something.

Up on one of the towering cliffs, a boy disguised as a clown was watching the pier through a telescope. 'Excellent,' he said, rubbing his hands together. 'Excellent indeed.'

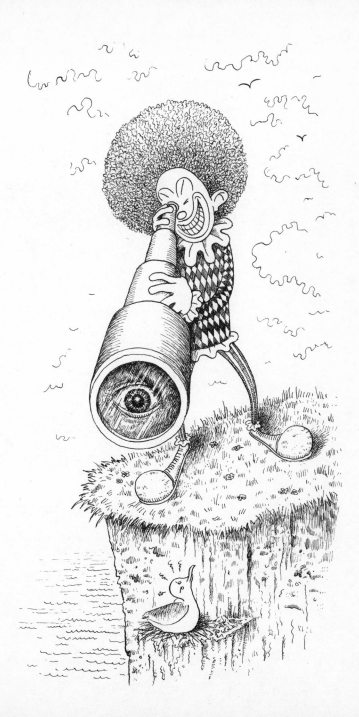

STRIPE EIGHT

The next morning, the gang of three and a bit woke up to feel themselves being rocked from side to side. 'I feel most queasy,' said Entelechy.

'I think we're at sea,' said Boyface.

They listened carefully. They could hear seagulls and water. They could hear the creaking of timber.

'I wonder where we are,' whispered Boyface.

'Why don't I sneak out,' suggested Clootie. 'Have a look around.'

'Okay,' agreed Boyface, nodding. 'But be careful. Don't get caught by any sailors.'

Clootie quickly put on her shoes.

'See if there's a decent bathroom somewhere,' stretched Entelechy. 'I could do with a soak.'

Clootie grabbed hold of the container's lid and pushed, but it wouldn't budge. She gave it a stronger push and a firm shove. But it was stuck fast. 'I think someone has locked us in,' she shouted.

The next five minutes were a little chaotic.

Clootie was the first to panic. She didn't like being in small dark spaces at the best of times, and very quickly her pushes became angry punches as she realised that she definitely hated being trapped in a crate on a strange boat.

Entelechy was usually pretty cool and very rarely lost his head. Whenever he did start to feel panicky, he simply sat himself in various yoga positions to calm himself down. And this is what he started to do. The only problem with this technique was that for some reason it irritated Clootie hugely. She just couldn't bear watching him twist his arms and legs into such weird shapes when they were in the middle of a crisis.

'Stop doing that, Entelechy,' Clootie shouted whilst trying to scrag the inside of the container's lid. 'It's not natural.'

'On the contrary,' panted Entelechy. 'It's the most natural thing in the world.'

The tension between the two was now putting the Tartan Badger on edge. It was chasing its tail, spinning faster and faster in a doughnut of multi-coloured fur.

All this was making Boyface's head hurt. This was the gang's first attempt at a proper adventure and it was rapidly turning into a disaster. This wasn't the power of three and a bit. This was more like the patheticness of three and a bit. He really wanted to get to Tropical Antarctica and rescue his dad. He desperately wanted his plan to work, but at that moment they were nothing more than three children and the worst pet in the whole wild world stuck in a box.

Eventually, of course, Clootie's shouting and punching attracted

some attention. Boyface was the
first to hear noises outside the crate.
'Shush,' he instructed the others.
They eventually shushed and held
their breaths, listening. They heard
footsteps. They heard the clanking
of metal on metal. They heard the
sound of voices. The voices were
talking to each other. No, not talking,
they were singing to each other.

'What's going on in that crate?' sang
one voice.

'I don't know and I really don't care,'
sang another.

'Sounds to me like it's full of kids.'

'Maybe we should open it up – take off the lid.'

Boyface didn't recognise the voices but something deep in his heart told him that he had heard them before. The gang of three and a bit sat very still as they heard the bolt being slid back across the outside of the crate.

The first thing Boyface noticed was that it was dark. Then he looked up and saw the top of a cliff looming above them. He wondered what foreign shore it could be. The next thing he saw was two hairy donkey faces, both wearing sailor hats.

'Umm... hello,' gulped Boyface. 'I'm Boyface Antelope and I'm a Stripemonger.'

'It's a pleasure to meet you,' sang the seadonkeys.

'You're the singing seadonkeys,' said Boyface. 'Sometimes we can hear you singing beneath the waves.'

'That's us,' sang one of them. 'But we don't just sing. We're also really good at running cargo-ships.'

'Why do you only deliver at night?' asked Clootie.

The seadonkeys shrugged. 'People get really freaked out when they see donkeys in charge of a boat.'

'Are we in lots of trouble for stowing away on your boat?' asked Boyface quietly.

'Not really,' sang the first donkey. 'You're just in a container, which is slightly odd. But not illegal.'

'Are we far, far out to sea?' asked Clootie.

'No. Not at all,' hummed the second donkey. 'You're not on our boat, you see. You're at the end of the pier.'

It turned out that they had only been asleep for a few hours and the motion of the waves rocking the pier had convinced them that they were

actually at sea. The seadonkeys' ship
was moored beside the pier.

'Why are you in a container, anyway?'
asked the donkeys.

The gang explained the story to the
seadonkeys. The creatures seemed
sympathetic so Boyface asked, 'Do
you think you could take us to Tropical
Antarctica to find my dad?'

The two seadonkeys looked at each
other. 'There wouldn't be a lot of
point,' they said. 'We didn't take him
to Tropical Antarctica.'

'But didn't you kidnap him?' asked Clootie forcefully, looking for a scrag.

The seadonkeys explained that yes, they did kidnap Mr Antelope but they only put him in one of the old crates at the end of the pier.

Some weird-clown-boy had given them some money to kidnap Mr Antelope and take him away. 'But that seemed a bit nasty,' said one of the seadonkeys. 'The weird-clown-boy said that Mr Antelope was a horrible, evil man who hated donkeys. We thought that the balanced thing to do was to stick him in a container to teach him a lesson but not take him to the other side of the world. And keep the clown's money. We'll do anything for money.'

'Mr Antelope is a lovely man,' Entelechy told them. 'He adores animals. He puts stripes on most of them.'

The gang of three and a bit climbed out of the container and had a look around. They were quite disappointed to see that they had never left the rickety pier at all. Boyface felt the stones wobble with the waves and smiled at how easy it would be to mistakenly think that you were on a boat. Boyface had a good look at the seadonkeys' ship. In the full moonlight he could just make out its name written on the side of its hull. The *Moules Mariniere*. He looked across at the beach and imagined Mr Antelope throwing a bottle into what he thought were distant waves but was really just the water by the pier.

'Which container is my dad in?' he asked the seadonkeys.

The donkeys pointed across the pier to the rusty old cuboid that they'd thrown his dad into.

'We'd better tell Dad that he's not half way to Tropical Antarctica after all.'

'Maybe the thing to learn from this mystery,' suggested Entelechy as they all skipped over to Boyface's dad, 'is that sometimes the thing you're looking for isn't on the other side of the world.'

'It's at the end of the pier.' completed Boyface.

Everyone was, of course, extremely happy to see Mr Antelope return to The Shop. He was a little thinner and quite pale. He looked like he could do with a fried egg sandwich.

Mrs Antelope had been unable to sleep that night and she'd been sitting on the roof looking out to sea. When she saw the gang of three and a bit walking up the street with her gorgeous husband, she was so excited she nearly fell off the roof. She ran down the stairs and met her beloved at the front door. They gave each other such a hug and a kiss that Boyface and the others had never seen anything like it in their lives.

The next day, a party was held in the café to celebrate Mr Antelope's return. Most of the village turned out to see him. Mandala Eyelash baked a special batch of scones and Shiny Tanker made a barbecue out of an old barrel.

The gang of three and a bit gathered around a table, shoving cream teas into their faces. 'How do you think we did on our first adventure together?' asked Clootie.

'We got back safely, I suppose,' shrugged Boyface.

'We got to meet some singing seadonkeys,' continued Entelechy.

'And you rescued me!' said Mr Antelope.

'It wasn't much of an adventure though, was it,' mused Boyface. 'We didn't even eat all those pancakes that Mum made.'

'I'm guessing, Entelechy,' said Daddy-This, 'that you didn't have time to spend any of that money we gave you, did you? Can I have it back?'

'Ah,' winced Entelechy. 'I did actually manage to spend that money. The singing seadonkeys had such charming hats that I just had to have one. And when I asked if they were for sale they said I could have two for the price of one. And I can't resist a bargain, so I bought them both.'

'And how much was the price of one?' asked Daddy-This.

'Exactly the amount of money that I had,' grinned Entelechy. 'Isn't that perfect?'

'You can't trust those seadonkeys,' tutted Mr Pointless. 'They'll do anything for money. It sounds like they took you for a ride.'

'I love a donkey ride,' said Mandala Eyelash.

When the party was over, everyone set off home. Everyone apart from Clootie Whanger who followed the Antelope family up the street. Her parents hadn't come to the party. Her parents never came to anything.

'Mr and Mrs Antelope?' she shouted nervously. 'I've got a bit of a problem.'

Mr and Mrs Antelope sat her down on a bench for a chat. 'What's the problem?' asked Mr Antelope.

'Well, I can't really go home. I don't think they're expecting me. I don't want to go home. I thought I was going to be away for months on an adventure to Tropical Antarctica. I told myself I was never coming back and I don't want to go back.'

'We could have a chat with your mum and dad, if you like,' suggested Mrs Antelope. 'See if they wouldn't mind you living with us for a while. I've always wanted a little girl. And Boyface could do with a sister.'

'Would I have to wear a saucepan on my head? Or a pillowcase? Or a cardboard box?'

'No,' breathed Mr Antelope with a smile. 'You wouldn't have to do any of that ever again.'

'But what about your bedroom, Clootie?' Boyface mumbled. 'You said that you could never live anywhere else because you love your bedroom so much.'

'That, young Stripemonger,' said Mrs
Antelope, rolling up her sleeves, 'is
my speciality.'

STRIPE TEN

Clootie's bedroom had soon been snapped off the Whangers' house and bodged on to the top of the Antelope family home. Mr and Mrs Antelope used the wrong sort of glue and some tools they had lying around that weren't really suitable for building with. Clootie's bedroom door was now only a couple of

corridors and a spiral staircase up from Boyface's bedroom.

That night, Boyface and his dad sat on the roof for a while. They couldn't see the sea because the clouds had rolled in and were just touching the chimney tops of the house. Boyface activated the Tartan Badger and used its bumhole to project his Stripemongering disasters onto the clouds that were hanging around them like damp friends. Boyface had recorded them with the Tartan Badger, and was able to play back the best bits so that Mr Antelope could catch up on what had happened while he was away.

'I'm glad you're back,' said Boyface. Boyface told his dad about the teenage pizza disaster and what he'd accidentally done to Maximilliana Muesli. Mr Antelope found it all a lot funnier than Boyface thought he would.

'The seadonkeys said that the weird-clown-boy paid them to kidnap you,' said Boyface. 'That's the same weird-clown-boy that poisoned the ponies with oranges and tried to blow up the Quantum Chromatic Disruption Machine. It's the same weird-clown-boy that kidnapped the Tartan Badger.'

'Yes,' nodded Mr Antelope. 'It looks to me like you have got yourself an enemy there. An arch-nemesis. I would imagine that you haven't heard the last of him. He'll be up in his hide-out, dreaming up new schemes.'

'With my gang of three and a bit, and you and Mum,' stumbled Boyface. 'I can outwit him, can't I?'

Mr Antelope looked at Boyface with a crinkled squint. 'You may have a gang and a Tartan Badger, Boyface,' he said seriously. 'And you might have a super-strong mum and a Stripemongering father. But it's not going to be easy.'

'Will I have to be sensibly responsible and responsibly sensible?' Boyface asked sheepishly.

'You will have to be much more than that,' whispered his dad. 'You will have to be magnificent!'

That night Boyface was curled up in bed with a book about Chromatic Algorithms. The Tartan Badger was asleep, alternately snoring and farting and smelling like the insides of an unwormed labradoodle.

'Good night, Boyface!' yelled Clootie from her bedroom.

'Good night, Clootie,' chuckled Boyface. He switched off his torch, went straight to sleep and dreamed his day all over again.

MR. ANTELOPE'S

GUIDE TO

COMPONENTS

OF THE

QUANTUM
CHROMATIC
DISRUPTION
MACHINE

VOLUME ONE

COMPONENTS

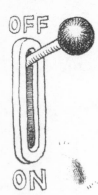

ON/OFF SWITCH:
NOT AS SIMPLE AS YOU MIGHT THINK. IT DOES
SWITCH THE MACHINE ON AND OFF, BUT NOT EVERY
TIME. SOMETIMES IT JUST MAKES LITTLE PURPLE
LIGHTS DO A KIND OF SAUSAGEY DANCE.

CLOCK:
THIS IS A REGULAR HOUSEHOLD CLOCK
THAT I PERSONALLY WIRED INTO THE SYSTEM.
IT NOT ONLY TELLS THE TIME
BUT GIVES YOU A WARNING IF YOU'VE
BEEN STARING AT THE OBSERVATION
PANEL FOR TOO LONG (BAD FOR YOUR EYES).

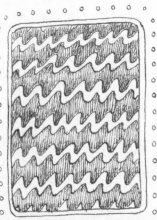

OBSERVATION PANEL:
THIS IS HOW WE CAN SEE WHAT'S GOING
ON INSIDE THE MACHINE WITHOUT
CLIMBING INSIDE IT AND ACCIDENTALLY
ENDING UP WITH STRIPY OR ELECTRIC HAIR.

THE LORENZA TRACTOR BEAM:

THIS CONTROLS PARTICLES AND PUTS THEM WHERE YOU WANT THEM, BUT IS VERY DIFFICULT TO KEEP A HANDLE ON AS IT RELIES ON CHAIN REACTIONS. IF WRONGLY OPERATED, THIS PART CAN ACCIDENTALLY SUCK THE UNIVERSE UP ITS OWN BOTTOM.

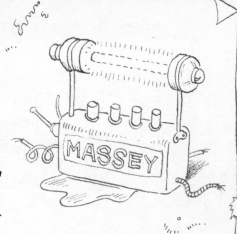

OPTICAL WIDENER LENS:

WHEN BOYFACE ASKS ME A DIFFICULT QUESTION ABOUT STRIPEMONGERING I USUALLY TELL HIM THAT MORE WILL BE REVEALED. THIS LENS ACTUALLY DOES THAT.

MAGNETWAFFLES:

THESE HELP US POSITION THE ZEBRA OR WHATEVER YOU HAVE PUT INTO THE MACHINE AND STABILISE IT SO THE PATTERN DOESN'T GET SMUDGED. WEIRDLY, THEY TASTE OF MAPLE SYRUP IF YOU LICK THEM.

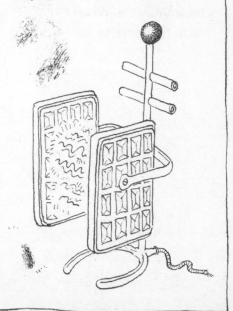

RAINBOW GENERATOR:
USES A PRISM, A MAGNIFYING GLASS AND A TINY ARK TO CREATE RAINBOWS OF DIFFERENT SHAPES AND SIZES.

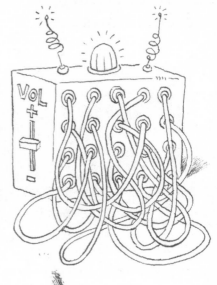

HYDRO-STATIC CHROMATIC FLUX INDUCTOR WITH OPTIONAL SPECTRUM GUARD AND 2000 MEGAMEGS GORILLASCOPE:
TURNS THE VOLUME UP AND DOWN.

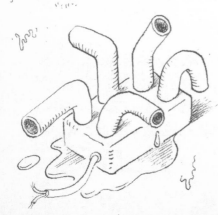

SPROCKET RELEASE HOUSING:
I HAVE NO IDEA WHAT THIS BIT IS FOR BUT I FIND ONE EVERY TIME I DO REPAIRS ON THE MACHINE.

QUANTUM GLUE GUN:
THIS FIRES A SPECIAL GLUE THAT
WORKS ON A SUB-ATOMIC LEVEL
(IT'S ACTUALLY DRIED CEREAL).

THATT'S REGULATOR:
THIS KEEPS PATTERNS REGULAR
AND STRIPES PARALLEL. IT
STOPS COLOURS GETTING TOO
WIDE AND DOTS BECOMING
TOO POINTY. IT ALSO STOPS
BOYFACE'S TROUSERS FROM
FLYING AWAY WHEN HE LETS
OFF A BOTTOM-BURP (DON'T
TELL HIM I SAID THAT).

IF YOU WOULD LIKE TO PUT TOGETHER YOUR OWN MAGICAL
MACHINE, YOU CAN GET MOST OF THESE COMPONENTS FROM ANY
GOOD ELECTRICAL STORE OR GO TO BOSUN & QUANTUM WHO HAVE
SHOPS ON MOST RETAIL PARKS AND WHOSE HEAD OFFICE IS IN
TROPICAL ANTARCTICA.

Enter the weird and wonderful world of Boyface.

'*Super funny*' GUARDIAN

www.thejamescampbell.com

Hodder
Children's
Books